Many thanks to Frédéric Rautzy for his invaluable help.
M. O.

Blue Dot Kids Press

www.BlueDotKidsPress.com

Original English-language edition published in 2022 by Blue Dot Kids Press,

PO Box 2344, San Francisco, CA 94126. Blue Dot Kids Press is a trademark of Blue Dot Publications LLC.

Original English-language edition © 2022 Blue Dot Publications LLC

Original English-language edition translation © 2022 Johanna McCalmont

Author and Illustrator: Marta Orzel

French-language edition originally published under the title:

Au parc il y a © Belin Jeunesse / Humensis, 2017. Translation rights arranged through Syllabes Agency,

France, and is published under exclusive license with Belin Jeunesse / Humensis.

Original English-language edition edited by Summer Dawn Laurie and designed by Teresa Bonaddio

BLUE D●T KIDS PRESS

Cataloging in Publication Data is available from the United States Library of Congress.

ISBN: 9781737603245

FSC
www.fsc.org
MIX
Paper from
responsible sources
FSC™ C136333

Printed in China with soy inks.

First Printing

MY DAY
in the
PARK

Marta Orzel

BLUE DOT KIDS PRESS

I love the park. Every day there is something new to discover.
Let's see what we find today!

Bandstand

Garden

Gardener's
shed

Greenhouse

Pond

Sky

Playground

Paths

Big lawn

Picnic area

Small
wood

Petting zoo

Entrance

At the entrance, I recognize lots of people . . .

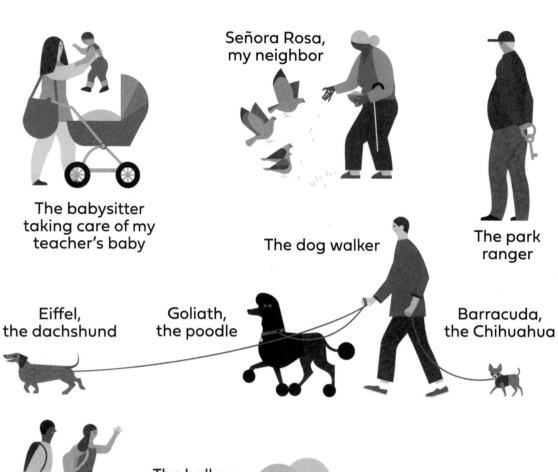

The babysitter taking care of my teacher's baby

Señora Rosa, my neighbor

The park ranger

The dog walker

Eiffel, the dachshund

Goliath, the poodle

Barracuda, the Chihuahua

Max and Mila, my friends from school

The balloon vendor

The man selling candy

The librarian reading a newspaper

The baker taking a nap

There's my best friend, Andy, the gardener's cat!
He is always here to greet us.

As I walk along the paths, I see lots of active people . . .

Bocce

Horseback riding

Jogging

Badminton

Frisbee

Hula-Hoop

Yoga

Soccer

Tai Chi

Basketball

Table tennis

I'm always excited (and a little scared)
to watch the tightrope walkers.

Down by the pond, I see a . . .

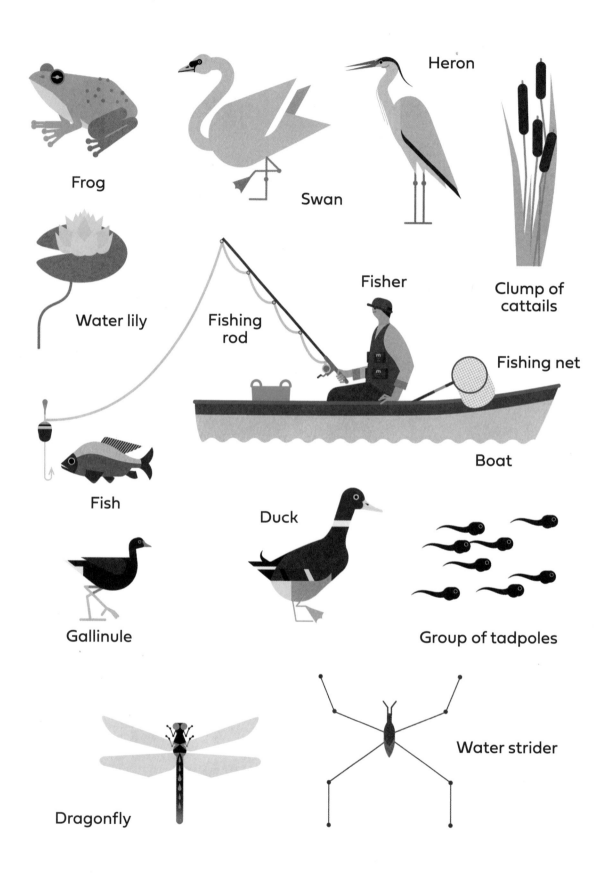

I love counting the ducklings swimming behind their mama.
How many are there today?

On the big lawn, I search for flowers and little creatures . . .

Bee

Wasp

Ladybug

Ant

Caterpillar

Beetle

Firebug

Snail

Earthworm

Buttercup

Daisy

Mole

Poppy

I make the same wish on a dandelion every visit.
Shh, it's a secret!

In the sky, I watch the birds as they fly . . .

Swallow

Chickadee

Owl

Pigeon

Sparrow

Seagull

Nightingale

Blackbird

Raven

Hawk

Robin

Woodpecker

It's a special surprise whenever I see a flock of
wild geese fly in a *V* formation.

In the small wood, I walk through the tall trees . . .

Cherry tree

Cherries

Chestnut tree

Chestnuts

Oak tree

Acorns

Pine tree

Pinecones

Apple tree

Apples

Squirrel

Hazelnuts

Chicks

Nest

How long will I be able to balance a
helicopter maple seed on my nose this time?

Time to eat! I look in the picnic basket for . . .

Lemonade

A glass

Applesauce

Pickles

A bottle of water

A sandwich

A slice of ham

A knife

A fork   A plate   A spoon

Carrot sticks

Chocolate cake

A chunk of stinky cheese

A slice of pizza

A bag of chips

Deviled eggs

Picnics are the best
because I get to eat
with my hands
(and share a little
with the ants).

In the greenhouse, I discover plants and birds
that live in tropical climates . . .

Cockatoo

Toucan

Pineapple

Papaya
plant

Banana
tree

Orchid

Coconut

Mango

Bamboo

Coffee plant

Prickly
pear
cactus

Palm
tree

I never
leave without a visit
to the butterfly garden.

At the playground, there are so many choices . . .

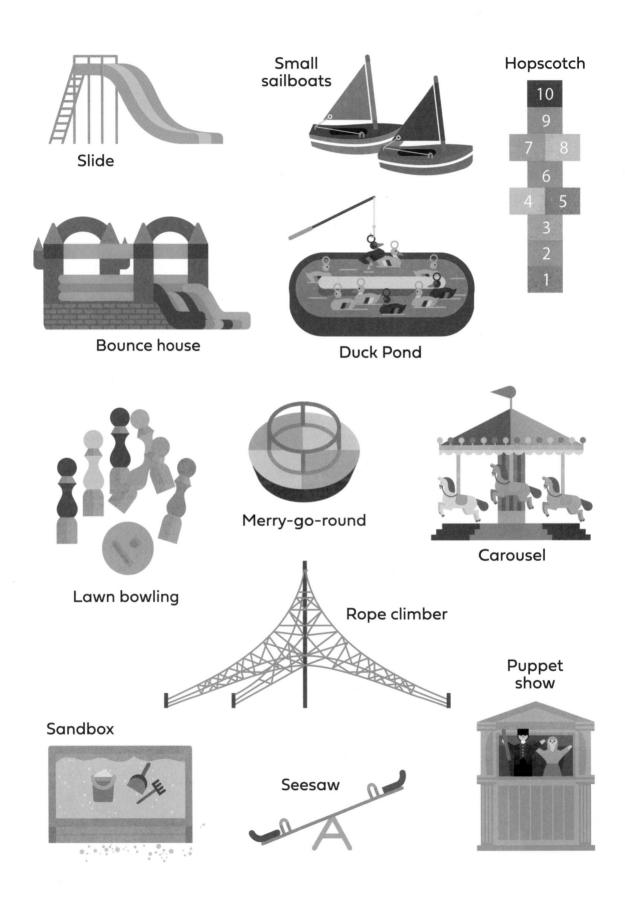

Slide

Small sailboats

Hopscotch

Bounce house

Duck Pond

Lawn bowling

Merry-go-round

Carousel

Rope climber

Sandbox

Seesaw

Puppet show

My headstand gets better the more I practice.

At the bandstand, I hear . . .

Cymbals

Castanets

Guitar

Ukulele

Harmonica

Maracas

Tambourine

Triangle

Banjo

Violin

Accordion

Xylophone

My favorite instrument
in the band is the big tuba.

In his shed, the gardener stores a . . .

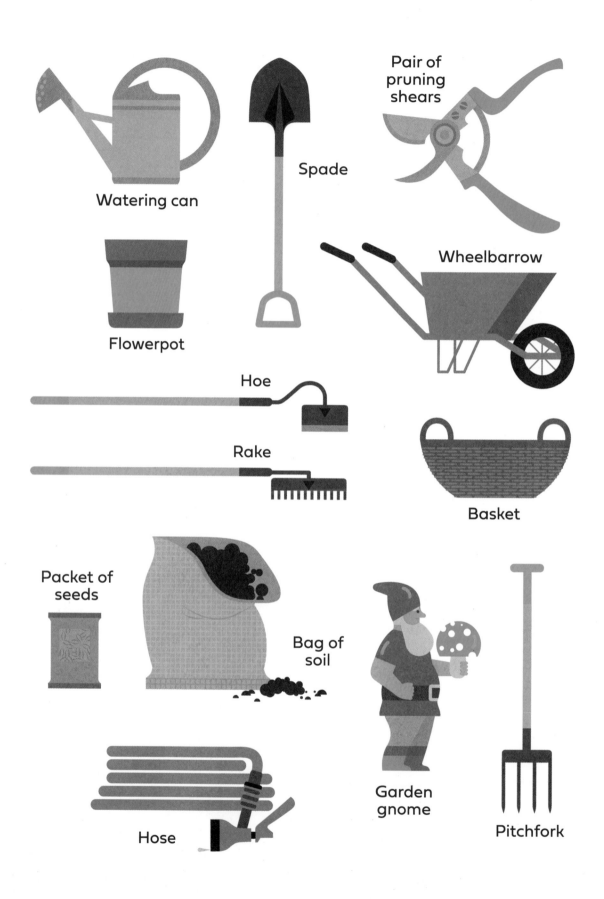

Watering can

Spade

Pair of pruning shears

Flowerpot

Wheelbarrow

Hoe

Rake

Basket

Packet of seeds

Bag of soil

Garden gnome

Pitchfork

Hose

Sometimes it takes a while to find the family of mice.
Today they are having a snack.

In the garden, I see many kinds of fruits and vegetables growing . . .

Green beans

Peas

Turnips

Beets

Raspberries

Strawberries

Carrots

Cauliflower

Leeks

Eggplants

Lettuce

Black currants

Red currants

Tomatoes

Potatoes

The pumpkins, spaghetti squash,
and cucumbers finally look ripe.

At the petting zoo, all sorts of animals roam . . .

Cow

Goat

Sheep

Pony

Horse

Rabbit

Goose

Rooster

Chicken

Donkey

Guinea fowl

Pig

Peacock

As soon as she sees me,
the llama comes to say hi.

Do you remember where in the park we saw these things?

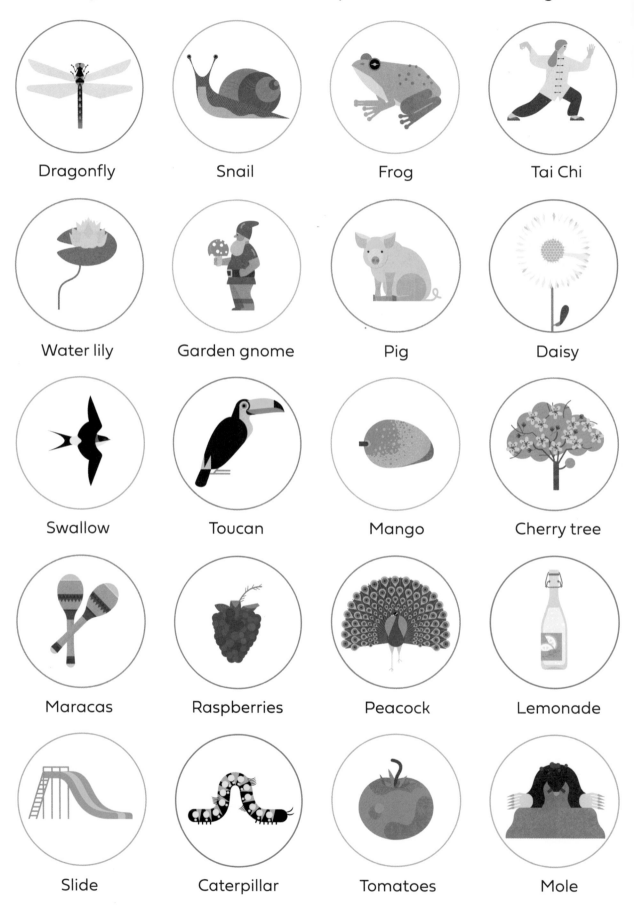

Dragonfly   Snail   Frog   Tai Chi

Water lily   Garden gnome   Pig   Daisy

Swallow   Toucan   Mango   Cherry tree

Maracas   Raspberries   Peacock   Lemonade

Slide   Caterpillar   Tomatoes   Mole

Wheelbarrow

Heron

Triangle

Turnips

Chicks in a nest

Red currants

Merry-go-round

Ant

Woodpecker

Andy

Señora Rosa

Hopscotch

Yoga

Ladybug

Hazelnuts

Violin

Orchid

Sheep

Scooter

Balloon vendor

What will we find in the park tomorrow?